YOU CHOOSE

CAN YOU
SAVE A TROPICAL
RAIN FOREST?

AN INTERACTIVE ECO ADVENTURE

BY ERIC BRAUN

CAPSTONE PRESS
a capstone imprint

You Choose Books are published by Capstone Press, an imprint of Capstone.
1710 Roe Crest Drive
North Mankato, Minnesota 56003
www.capstonepub.com

Library of Congress Cataloging-in-Publication Data
Names: Braun, Eric, 1971– author.
Title: Can you save a tropical rain forest? : an interactive eco adventure / by Eric Braun.
Description: North Mankato, Minnesota : Capstone Press, [2021] | Series: You choose : eco expeditions | Includes bibliographical references and index. | Audience: Ages 8–11 | Audience: Grades 4–6
Identifiers: LCCN 2020039307 (print) | LCCN 2020039308 (ebook) | ISBN 9781496695994 (hardcover) | ISBN 9781496697073 (paperback) | ISBN 9781977153944 (eBook PDF)
Subjects: LCSH: Rain forest conservation--Juvenile literature. | Forest canopies—Conservation—Juvenile literature. | Endangered species—Conservation—Juvenile literature.
Classification: LCC SD411 .B73 2021 (print) | LCC SD411 (ebook) | DDC 333.75—dc23
LC record available at https://lccn.loc.gov/2020039307
LC ebook record available at https://lccn.loc.gov/2020039308

Summary: The world's tropical rain forests are being destroyed. But you can help! Navigate through three different stories in this rain forest rescue mission. With dozens of possible outcomes, it's up to you to save the rain forests before they disappear forever. The planet needs you. Will YOU CHOOSE to help?

Editorial Credits
Editors: Michelle Parkin and Aaron Sautter; Designer: Bobbie Nuytten; Media Researcher: Kelly Garvin; Production Specialist: Katy LaVigne

Photo Credits
Alamy: Nigel Dickinson, 17, Stock Connection Blue, 10: Dreamstime/Eakklik Aumaon, 69; Getty Images/NurPhoto, 28; iStockphoto: dsongrandisoli, 83, xp33gt, 34; Minden Pictures: Christian Ziegler, 52-53, Mark Moffett, 60: Newscom: David Woodfall/ZUMA Press, 80, Erik de Castro, 104-105; Science Source/Jessica Wilson/NASA, 106-107; Shutterstock: AB Photographie, 107 (bottom middle), Arnain, 100, Bene_A, 107 (top right), Bildagentur Zoonar GmbH, 106 (bottom right), Bumble Dee, 38, Chokniti Khongchum, 86, costas anton dumitrescu, 73, Dr Morley Read, 91, edeantoine, 42, Edwin Butter, 106 (bottom left), G.J. Verspui, 93, GUDKOV ANDREY, 66, 107 (bl), 107 (br), j.woootthisak, 98, Mabelin Santos, 6, Mark Green, 106 (tl), Michael Lynch, 77, neelsky, 107 (tl), Ondrej Prosicky, 55, Rich Carey, 63, Sergey Uryadnikov, cover (top), 1 (t), 50, Toa55, cover (bottom), backcover (t), 1 (b), 4, 23, 31, Travel Stock, 44

Design Elements:
Shutterstock/tonia_tkach

All internet sites appearing in back matter were available and accurate when this book was sent to press.

TABLE OF CONTENTS

ABOUT YOUR ADVENTURE

YOU are a researcher trying to save the tropical rain forests from extinction. With your team of dedicated scientists, can you help save them before it's too late?

Chapter One sets the scene. Then you choose which path to read. Follow the directions at the bottom of the page as you read the stories. The decisions you make will change your outcome. After you finish one path, go back and read the others for new perspectives and more adventures.

Turn the page to begin your adventure.

The Punta Culebra Nature Center is part of the Smithsonian Tropical Research Institute in Panama City, Panama. The institute studies animals and plants living in tropical regions and the impacts of human activity on them.

CHAPTER 1

TROPICAL FOREST SCIENTIST

You peer out the window as your plane banks over the Pacific Ocean. The water below is vast and blue. It sparkles in the afternoon sun. As the plane turns toward the Panama Airport, your stomach does flip-flops. Today is an exciting day. You've been preparing a long time for this.

You've been studying tropical forests and how to save them for your whole career. Now you are traveling to a research center in Panama. There, you will meet with researchers and world-renowned scientists who are doing important work with tropical forests and marine ecosystems. You'll also get your first big assignment.

Turn the page.

You see the forest canopy below you now. Then it clears, the runway appears, and the plane touches down with a lurch. At last, you have arrived.

A Panamanian researcher meets you at the gate. He has shaggy hair, friendly eyes, and a big smile.

"Bienvenidos a Panama!" he says, using the Spanish word for "welcome." He gives you a friendly handshake and introduces himself as Eduardo. "But you can call me Eddie," he says.

Eddie takes your bags and places them into his old station wagon. Then you are off to the research center. You roll down your window and let the hot, humid air wash over you. When you arrive at the center, Eddie takes you to a dorm room where you'll stay the night. You drop off your duffel bag, and the two of you get a bite to eat in the cafeteria.

"You have come at a great time," Eddie says with a big smile. "There are so many important projects going on now, you are sure to learn a lot. And we can use your help."

After dinner, you stroll the grounds, checking out the state-of-the-art lab facilities. Later, you meet several of the scientists in a conference room. Eddie and the others discuss three projects that you can join. You will leave first thing in the morning. Which one will you choose?

To fight tropical forest fires raging in Brazil in South America, turn to page 11.

To work on a canopy project in the Democratic Republic of the Congo in Africa, turn to page 43.

To work with endangered animals, turn to page 67.

In South America, large areas of the rain forest are often burned to make room for farmland.

CHAPTER 2

FIREFIGHT

Eddie and an American researcher named Nora are joining you on your journey to Brazil. Like Eddie, Nora is passionate about the work being done to save the tropical forests. But she knows that fighting fires is dangerous work.

"Especially," Nora says dryly, "if we meet people who *want* the fires to burn."

You shake your head sadly. You know the people in these rain forests are in a difficult situation.

A small propeller plane takes you to Manaus, Brazil. On the way, you manage to get a little sleep, but you wake up when you hear Nora whisper, "Oh!" Out the window, the sky is dark, though it is still the middle of the afternoon.

Turn the page.

"It's worse than I imagined," Nora says.

"Buckle up!" calls the pilot. "This could get bumpy!"

You fly into the smoke, the little plane rocking and rattling in the wind. Below, you can see flares lighting a runway in the dark.

At last you land at the airport in Manaus, and you let out a sigh of relief. But the smoky air makes you choke. You drive a couple hours, deep into the forest to an emergency base. You can only see a couple dozen feet through the smoke.

At the base, you meet a man named Antonio. Eddie tells you that Antonio always knows when there's trouble. It's like he can smell it.

Antonio explains the situation. Ranchers and farmers are burning sections of the Amazon forest to make room for raising livestock and crops. The burning is being encouraged by politicians who are supported by the agricultural companies. But the loss of the huge, ancient trees causes severe damage to the environment. The trees store massive amounts of carbon dioxide. When the trees are gone, the carbon is released back into the atmosphere. Earth heats up faster. Climate change gets worse.

Antonio tells you that he needs help in two different areas right now.

"We have airplanes dumping fire retardant on the flames from above. We need crews to help in the sky," Antonio says. "We also need people on the ground building firebreaks in the woods to slow the spread of the flames."

Eddie and Nora look to you. It's your call.

To join an airplane crew, turn to page 14.
To work in the woods, turn to page 16.

Flying through the smoke when you arrived in Manaus was scary. But you have to admit, it was thrilling too. You decide to work on the plane.

You, Eddie, and Nora find yourselves on a runway once again, looking at an airplane. This time it's a DC-7, an air tanker that will carry and drop fire retardant. The mixture is made of water and a type of fertilizer that soaks into wood, making it harder to burn. A pilot is teaching you what to do. It's a lot to remember. Your mind is whirling. You hope you can remember all of this technical information. Just as the lesson is winding up, an airport guard quickly rushes up to your group.

"You better not go up!" he says. "There's a local militia that has vowed to keep the fires blazing. We think someone may have gotten through and tampered with the planes."

"I've been with this plane all day," the pilot, Jenay, says. She wears a flight suit and already is pulling on her helmet. "Nobody has tampered with it."

"I wouldn't be so sure," the guard says.

The pilot stares at the guard. "We have to put out these fires," she says.

To go up in the plane, turn to page 20.
To ask for an inspection of the plane, turn to page 22.

You've had enough flying through flame-licked skies for one day. You tell Antonio that you'll do ground duty. You, Nora, and Eddie climb into an old pickup truck.

Nora takes the wheel. "Let's do this!" she says.

A flatbed trailer truck pulls up behind you. It has a big bulldozer on its bed. Nora gets directions from Antonio, double-checks the map he gave her, and pulls away from the camp. You bounce on the seat as you move through the trees on a bumpy road. The flatbed follows behind slowly, the bulldozer on the back clipping tree branches as it goes.

Your mission is to build firebreaks. Using the bulldozer, saws, and other equipment, you'll cut down trees to create wide, open areas. The empty land will take away the fire's fuel. With nothing else to burn, it will eventually go out.

Turn the page.

Bulldozers are often used to help build fire breaks in rain forests. The fire breaks help keep fires from spreading.

The dark smoke is thicker than ever. You can only see a few feet ahead of you, and Nora is driving very slowly. Finally she pulls the truck into a small clearing and climbs out. You can hear the fire raging nearby. Birds fly past, looking for safety. Suddenly a dark figure appears in the smoky clearing. It is a farmer dressed in simple clothes.

"*Olá!*" the farmer calls. It means hello in Portuguese.

Eddie walks up to the man and speaks with him in Portuguese. Then he comes back to you and Nora.

"The farmer is asking for our help. He's desperate to keep the fires burning," Eddie says. "His family is starving. But if the land is cleared, he can farm it. He can make money."

"We can't help him," Nora says. "We're here to put out the fire."

After Eddie relays this message, the man walks in front of the bulldozer. He lies down on the road, blocking its path.

To try talking to the farmer, turn to page 25.
To try scaring him off, turn to page 27.

"I trust you," you say to the pilot. "Let's get in the air."

Eddie goes to another, smaller plane. This will be the spotter. It will fly ahead of you, going higher and farther, to identify where your plane needs to drop retardant. Eddie will radio to you in the air tanker and tell you where to go.

You and Nora climb into the DC-7 and take off. Black plumes of smoke rise above the trees, forming a dark pillow in the sky. Your plane flies just below it. You are sandwiched between the heat of the fires below and the cloud of smoke above.

Eddie comes over the radio and gives the coordinates for your first dump. Jenay radios back and turns the plane. She flies even lower. You feel like you could reach down and touch the treetops.

"Here's our spot!" Jenay yells at you.

You grab the handle and get ready to release a heavy stream of retardant. But suddenly the plane hits a pocket of wind and drops hard. The next thing you know, your head is bleeding.

Jenay is yelling, "Now! Now!"

You realize that in your rush to get going, you forgot to put on your safety belt. So did Nora. The plane bucks again and all three of you are jerked violently. Nora is tossed onto the floor.

"Drop it now!" Jenay yells again.

To try to get your safety belt on, turn to page 29.
To pull the lever first, turn to page 31.

The guard's face says it all—he's scared. He really thinks someone did something to the plane. And that makes *you* scared too.

"We'd better get a mechanic over here to check out the plane," you say.

"There's no time for that!" the pilot says. "The forest is burning!"

"If the plane goes down, we can't help at all," you say.

"I agree," Nora says. "We'd better get it checked."

You find Antonio and tell him what happened. It takes two hours before a mechanic is free. Finally he comes over. He scours the engine compartment, but soon Antonio calls him to another job—an emergency. The mechanic shrugs and heads off.

By this time, the pilot is furious. She is pacing around the airfield yelling into a cell phone. It's another hour before the mechanic returns. When he finishes his inspection, it is late at night. The fires have gained strength and are dangerously close.

Turn the page.

Despite the efforts of brave firefighters, millions of acres of rain forest have been burned in South America.

Your first flight will be fighting fires that are only a few miles from the camp. If you can't get them under control, the entire operation may have to move. The good news is there is nothing wrong with the engine.

As you, Nora, and the pilot climb aboard, the pilot turns to you. "I just hope we haven't lost too much time," she snarls.

So do I, you think.

THE END

To read another adventure, turn to page 9.
To learn more about Tropical Rain Forests, turn to page 101.

You and Eddie walk over to where the farmer is lying in the dirt. With Eddie translating, you ask about his family. He talks about his wife. He tells you about his two daughters. They are smart girls with plans to go to college—something he never got to do.

"Think of how much they will miss you if you are killed doing this," you say. Eddie translates.

You talk for another 10 minutes. Finally the farmer sighs and gets up. You must have gotten through to him. He walks back into the trees.

Working quickly now, the bulldozer pushes through the trees. You, Nora, and Eddie begin cutting logs and hauling them aside. You have been working for only a few minutes when the bulldozer plunges through the ground into a hole. The back end of its tracks pokes up.

Turn the page.

The driver climbs out of the machine. "The hole was hidden with branches," he says angrily. "Someone must have been working on it while that farmer was stalling us."

You get a prickly feeling on the back of your neck, as if you're being watched. Is someone still here? The fire is roaring even louder. It's getting close. But you can't do anything with the bulldozer in the pit.

To hook up a cable from the flatbed and pull the bulldozer out, turn to page 33.

To give up on the bulldozer and get to safety, turn to page 36.

Maybe you can scare the farmer away. You tell the driver to fire up the bulldozer. The farmer flinches, but doesn't move. Nora is furious. She takes it a step further.

"Let's see how brave he is with that monster breathing down his throat," she says.

Nora signals to the driver, and the bulldozer begins crawling toward the farmer. The farmer lies there staring down the machine. He's crying, but he doesn't move. For him, this means his family's survival.

Suddenly you step in front of the bulldozer.

"Stop!" you yell.

You won't let the bulldozer get any closer. You signal the driver to take the bulldozer back to the flatbed.

Turn the page.

Firefighters in South America often work long hours in difficult conditions and carry heavy gear to battle forest fires.

You'll have to drive back to the basecamp and check in with Antonio. Maybe he knows a way to help the farmer *and* save the forest.

THE END

To read another adventure, turn to page 9.
To learn more about Tropical Rain Forests, turn to page 101.

If you hit those trees without a safety belt on, you could die. So you reach for the belt. It takes a couple seconds because your hands are trembling. But finally, you are safely strapped in.

The plane clips the tops of the trees and bucks like a wild horse. Your body strains against the belt. Jenay pulls up, but she's angry at you for not releasing the retardant.

"You missed our chance!" she says.

You know Jenay is angry but you don't regret putting on your safety belt. And the second time Jenay passes over the fire, you pull it off perfectly. Her anger eases.

As you're flying back to the airfield, Jenay yawns. A moment later, she actually nods off, her head tipping down before she startles awake again. She sees you looking and laughs.

Turn the page.

"It's been a long day," Jenay says. "I've been flying for 16 hours."

You know that's more than the number of hours she is allowed to fly for safety reasons. This is intense work. After a certain number of hours, a pilot becomes too tired to fly. But once you're on the ground, she takes the plane over to get it loaded with more fire retardant. She wants to go back out.

To try to stop the pilot from going up again, turn to page 37.

To keep your mouth shut, turn to page 40.

Ignoring your own safety, you pull the lever. As you do, the plane hits a pocket of air, and you are tossed against the fuselage. Your wrist burns with pain, and you can't straighten your fingers.

Up front, Jenay yells out, "Awesome job!"

Turn the page.

Specialized airplanes and helicopters are often used to drop water or fire retardant chemicals over forest fires.

The retardant went exactly where it was supposed to. You climb onto your seat and try to buckle in with your good hand. Nora helps you. Your wrist is throbbing, but you keep working. You complete three more passes, dumping retardant on the spots Eddie directs you to on the radio. Each one is a success.

When you get back to the airfield, Jenay puts her hand up for a high five. But your wrist hurts too much to raise your hand. You find the medical tent, where a nurse tends to your sprained wrist and wraps your bleeding head. You'll have to go to the hospital in Manaus for tests on your head wound.

For now, the battle against the fires will go on without you. But one thing is for sure: You will be back.

THE END

To read another adventure, turn to page 9.
To learn more about Tropical Rain Forests, turn to page 101.

The flatbed truck is driven up to the pit. You grab the cable that comes off the back and climb down into the hole. You hook it to the bulldozer. The flatbed starts to back away. A few minutes later, the bulldozer is out.

Working around the hole, the bulldozer begins to push down trees. Branches whip your arms and cut your skin as you haul a log into the woods. Bugs fly into your mouth. The smoke makes you cough and hack. You're sweating so much that you can't grip your chainsaw.

Soon, Eddie hollers something to you. But you can't make it out over the noise of the trucks and crackling wood. He points, and you see the fire raging nearby. But you have to complete this firebreak—it's the perfect spot to save a big swath of the forest.

"Keep going!" you yell. "We're almost done!"

Turn the page.

But you feel dizzy. You fall down.

When you wake up, Nora is dragging you to the pickup truck. Trees crackle and burst like bombs. She pulls you into the truck and drives away from the hottest part of the fire.

Firefighters risk their lives every day to help save rain forests across South America.

"Where's Eddie?" you ask.

She glances over her shoulder, and you look out the back window. In the bed of the truck, Eddie lies on his back. The whole left side of his body is badly burned. Flames enclose the road behind you. You just make it out with your lives.

Later, lying in the medical tent, you learn that your efforts saved a lot of forest. But Eddie is in intensive care at the hospital in Manaus. It doesn't look good. As you're lying in the medical tent that night, you can't help but wonder if it was worth it.

THE END

To read another adventure, turn to page 9.
To learn more about Tropical Rain Forests, turn to page 101.

It's just too dangerous. You've heard stories about people with guns in these woods defending the fires. Even now it feels like there are eyes watching you in the woods.

You tell the crew that it's time to leave. You leave the bulldozer where it is in the hole and drive back to the base. When you pull in, Antonio walks over to you.

"That spot you left is not going to make it," Antonio says sadly. "Helicopter pilots are reporting that the damage is bad. We think hundreds of acres will be burnt by morning."

You'll never know if it would have been safe to stay and fight the fire. This is hard, dangerous work. But looking at all the disappointed faces, you wonder if you made the right choice to leave.

THE END

To read another adventure, turn to page 9.
To learn more about Tropical Rain Forests, turn to page 101.

"Jenay," you say sternly. "You need to get some sleep."

She glares at you with fire in her eyes equal to the fire in the woods. "Can't you see what's happening here?" she says. "Every moment that I'm not in the air, more forest burns."

Suddenly you see Antonio walking your way. You remember what Eddie said about Antonio— he can smell trouble. You suspect Antonio already knew that Jenay was over her flight hours limit.

When he arrives, Antonio puts his hand on Jenay's shoulder.

"Go get some rest," he tells her. She starts to protest, but he raises his hand in a "stop" gesture.

After Jenay goes to her tent, Antonio turns to you. "You'll be going up with another pilot," he says. You follow him to another plane.

Turn the page.

Highly skilled pilots need many hours of training to fly low over trees and spray fire retardant on forest fires.

Over the next few days, you go up many more times—sometimes with Jenay, sometimes with other pilots. You love the excitement of flying through flaming skies and fighting the fires. You become friends with Jenay. In a little over a week, the fires in this region are under control. Antonio asks if you'd like to join the crews moving farther south. Jenay tells you she will be going.

"Then I am too," you say.

THE END

To read another adventure, turn to page 9.
To learn more about the rain forest, turn to page 101.

You already made Jenay angry once. It was not a pleasant experience. Plus, you know how important this work is. So you bite your tongue about the hours. Back at the base, mechanics refill the air tanker with fire retardant. Jenay sits in her seat and nods off for a few minutes. Soon a mechanic calls out that the tank is full. Jenay opens her eyes slowly, rubs them, and turns to you.

"Ready?" she asks.

"Are *you* ready?" you ask tentatively.

"I'm always ready," she says.

She flips a couple switches, and the engine fires up. The noise fills the cabin as Jenay takes the big tanker toward the runway strip for takeoff. She says something else to you, but you can't hear her over the noise of the engine.

"What?" you yell.

"I said, buckle up this time!" Jenay yells.

I definitely will, you think.

THE END

To read another adventure, turn to page 9.
To learn more about Tropical Rain Forests, turn to page 101.

The rivers and thick jungles of central Africa are home to thousands of native plant and animal species.

CHAPTER 3
CANOPY LIFE

You and Eddie arrive in the Democratic Republic of the Congo ready to explore the rain forest canopy. Until recently, little was known about the rich plant and animal life in the canopy near the Congo River in central Africa. That's because the dense layer of the forest is hard to access so high above the ground. Even with new research methods, including airships, built-in walkways, and high-tech climbing equipment, progress has been slow. There is much to be learned. The canopy remains mysterious.

Recently a natural gas pipeline was built through the forest. The access roads built to install it damaged a huge amount of plant life— especially the trees themselves. Many animals have had their habitats damaged or destroyed.

Turn the page.

Your job is to find out how this has changed life for the plants and animals in the forest.

You and Eddie drive deep into the forest in a topless Jeep, bouncing on rough, narrow roads. You splash through massive puddles left over from that afternoon's rain. Monkeys howl and birds chirp. Soon you arrive at a small research center, the nerve center for a team of more than 30 researchers. The center bustles with energy.

Human-built roads cause a lot of damage in Africa's rain forests.

You and Eddie are assigned to a local scientist named Yohan. He'll assist you when you head out into the field.

Yohan shakes your hand and says, "I hope you're not afraid of heights."

Eddie breaks into a big smile, and so do you. "Let's find out," you say.

"Okay," Yohan says. "How do you want to approach the canopy? We can drive into the forest and climb up. Or we can fly overhead and drop down."

To enter the canopy from the air, turn to page 46.
To enter from the ground, turn to page 48.

You, Eddie, and Yohan climb aboard the helicopter with the pilot, stowing your gear in the back compartment. A big vinyl object is crumpled beneath the helicopter and secured by cables. The engine whistles to life, and the helicopter blades begin to spin.

Flying low over the forest, you are struck by the beauty of the treetops. Your imagination starts to race, thinking about all the life that teems below. The pilot lowers the craft into the treetops.

Once he steadies the helicopter over the trees, the pilot releases the cables holding the bundle of vinyl. As it falls, it unfolds and begins to inflate. Over the next few minutes, it blows up into a pretzel-shaped balloon. A tight net is stretched across it.

You, Eddie, and Yohan rappel down ropes onto the balloon. The helicopter flies away.

You get to work carefully securing the edges to the trees. You don't want the ropes to damage any branches. In the center of the raft is a trap door. You unlatch it and dangle your feet into the opening.

You have two main research goals here—to collect insect samples for testing and to install cameras in the canopy to monitor the movement of wildlife. Eddie has volunteered to head up the insect collecting. Yohan will work on installing cameras. You can join either one.

To work with Yohan installing cameras, turn to page 50.
To work with Eddie collecting insects, turn to page 57.

You, Eddie, and Yohan drive into the forest, using the maintenance roads built by the gas company. Eventually you reach a clearing and set up your tents.

Once everything is ready to go, you put on a nylon harness and helmet. Yohan uses a giant slingshot to shoot a climbing line into the trees, then climbs up. He secures rope attachments and sets up a pulley system. He drops a line to you. You hook it to your harness and begin to climb.

Slowly but steadily, the three of you climb up the tree to dizzying heights. When you reach the canopy, you find a pocket of rich soil in a joint between branches. You collect a sample and slip it into your shoulder bag. Eddie waves a butterfly net and catches a swarm of flying insects. Then he carefully transfers them to his own shoulder bag.

After a couple of hours, you take a break. The three of you hang happily in your harnesses, hundreds of feet up.

"We have tracked a leopard through this area," Yohan says. "I think it uses these upper branches as a sort of highway. I'd love to see that thing up close again."

You're about to follow him up when you notice a dark branch above you that seems to vibrate in the shadows.

"What is that?" you say to yourself.

To check out the strange dark branch, turn to page 52.
To follow Yohan to the leopard highway, turn to page 55.

You follow Yohan through the trap door, wearing your harness and climbing gear. He leads you to a nearby tree and tells you where to hang the first camera.

"This has always been a high-traffic area for bonobos," Yohan says. "If the pipeline has not damaged their habitat too much, this camera should capture the bonobos moving through here."

Bonobos are also known as pygmy chimpanzees. Wild bonobos only live in the rain forest in the Democratic Republic of Congo, Africa.

You move on to the next tree. You adjust your gear and swing across a gap in the branches. Here, Yohan has marked a spot for the next camera. It will overlook a long branch that reaches across a clearing above the pipeline. Like the previous spot, many animals use it as a bridge.

You carefully climb around to the far side of the wide tree trunk to get the best spot for the camera. But there isn't a good place to stand. You could hang the camera here where it's easier and try to tilt the lens toward the bridge. But you might not get the best photos.

To try to install the camera in the critical spot, turn to page 59.

To install it in the easier spot, turn to page 61.

You hoist yourself up to the strange, dark branch and secure your harness. Then you grab a scraping tool from your belt to get a sample. Just as you're about to touch the slippery-looking surface, Yohan calls to you.

"Careful!" he shouts.

But it's too late. Several large ants have already climbed onto your hand and are marching up your arm. You shake your hand, but the ants move up to your neck. Suddenly, you feel a seething pain—they're biting you!

Ant swarms in the rain forest can include up to 20 million individual army ants.

You scream and let go of your rope, slipping down more than a story before your safety harness catches and you jerk to a halt. Your head snaps painfully to the side.

Yohan hurries over. Ants are inside your clothes. They're crawling all over, biting, moving, and biting again. The pain is incredible.

"You're having an allergic reaction!" Yohan says.

The two of you climb back up your ropes, but you keep slipping. Yohan is working twice as hard to support himself and help you.

Turn the page.

At last, Yohan gives you a boost through the raft's trap door. While you lie on the net squinting in the sun, Yohan radios for the helicopter to come and get you. Soon you hear the helicopter's thwacking blades in the distance. You close your eyes.

Make the pain stop, you think, just before passing out.

THE END

To read another adventure, turn to page 9.
To learn more about Tropical Rain Forests, turn to page 101.

The idea of a leopard highway is too cool to pass up. You hurry after Yohan. You climb for several minutes before Yohan stops. You listen. There is a buzzing noise coming from somewhere. At first you think it is a swarm of insects, but the sound is mechanical. It is machinery.

Turn the page.

Leopards are normally solitary animals that are active at night. It is uncommon to spot one during the day.

You and the team creep across several trees, making your way toward the noise. You rappel to the ground and walk quickly along an access road toward the sound.

Eventually you approach a curve in the road. You know what is around the corner: heavy logging machines. The pipeline is finished. It is illegal to clear more trees. Yohan shakes his head sadly at the idea of more trees lost.

"We need to stop them," Yohan says. "But we must be careful. They could be armed."

To confront the loggers, turn to page 63.
To return to camp and radio back to the research center, turn to page 65.

You'd love to help learn more about the insects in the rain forest. You decide to join Eddie collecting specimens. But when you catch up to Eddie, he's frozen in his tracks. You follow his gaze to a tree 20 feet across. There, an animal is eating some leaves and looking at you.

"It's a bonobo," Eddie whispers. It looks a lot like a chimpanzee but with longer arms.

You know something about bonobos. They are the closest living relative to humans. And they are endangered.

The bonobo keeps looking at you. Then as you watch, you notice another bonobo appear in the shadows. And then another. And another. The more you stare, the more you see.

You and Eddie sit still, watching them. After a while, one of the animals turns and climbs with

Turn the page.

grace and speed, up and away. Another follows. Then they all go. Suddenly the forest feels quiet. You feel lucky to have seen them.

You spend the rest of the day collecting insects, but the big news of the day is the bonobo sighting. You can't wait to let the other researchers know. Maybe a new project will focus on counting them. You hope you will be a part of it.

THE END

To read another adventure, turn to page 9.
To learn more about Tropical Rain Forests, turn to page 101.

You're here to do a job, so you're going to do it. You toss a line over a branch above you and move around the tree trunk. You work your way to the far side of the trunk with nothing to stand on—just the rope above you to hold on to.

You secure the rope under your hips as a sort of seat and push your feet against the bark. Carefully, you reach into your pack and pull out the ball joint that will hold the camera. But as you reach out to the trunk, the joint slips. You try to grab it, but it falls.

You look down. Suddenly your foot slips. You fall forward, smacking your head on the tree as the rope slips out from under you. The bark scrapes your face, and you crash through a net of branches.

Turn the page.

Researchers often go to great lengths and risk their own safety to find and study wildlife in the rain forest.

You fall two stories to the forest floor. You think that your leg is broken. Your head hurts. All you can hear is a whistling sound inside your head. You can't move. You hope Yohan will find you soon—before a jungle animal does.

THE END

To read another adventure, turn to page 9.
To learn more about Tropical Rain Forests, turn to page 101.

You're not risking your life to get a few photos. So you secure the camera to this side of the tree trunk where you can stand on a solid branch. You angle the lens toward the bridge as best you can. You test the view on your phone, which is hooked up to the camera feed. You can see most of the bridge. It'll have to do.

That night you, Yohan, and Eddie settle in to the net shelter. You watch the forest night life on your phones, switching between the six cameras you set up that day. You see three leopards go across one of the bridges. You see a brush-tailed porcupine waddle across another bridge. You see a critically endangered gorilla. It is amazing to see what is happening below you in the canopy. The next day, you hang six more cameras.

Weeks later, camera footage reveals that leopard movement has decreased on the bridges.

Turn the page.

That means groups of leopards are separated from one another.

The research center makes a plan to build bridges across the pipeline. This should help increase the leopard population in the area. Your work has played an important role in possibly saving these animals.

THE END

To read another adventure, turn to page 9.
To learn more about Tropical Rain Forests, turn to page 101.

The three of you walk around the bend in the road. In the clearing before you, a huge tractor with a long arm is swinging a bundle of logs toward a truck bed. Several men work on logs with chainsaws. One of them sees you and turns his machine off. The others turn theirs off as well. The tractor cuts its engine too. It is suddenly very quiet. One of the men walks up to you.

Turn the page.

Logging and mining activity is destroying huge areas of the world's rain forests.

Yohan says something to him in Congolese. The man answers. He sounds angry. He pulls out a machete from behind his back. The other men walk closer.

Yohan backs up. When he reaches you and Eddie, he says, "We need to go now."

You see fear in his eyes, and you realize you are in danger. You back out of the clearing, never turning your back to the men. They follow you with their eyes. As soon as you reach the edge of the clearing, you turn and run as fast as you can. You hope you can outrun them.

THE END

To read another adventure, turn to page 9.
To learn more about Tropical Rain Forests, turn to page 101.

Out here in the forest, you're far from help. It's not wise to confront the loggers here, where anything can happen—and nobody would know.

So you go back to camp and pack up the Jeep. That afternoon, you report the logging. You point to the location on a GPS device. The other researchers are furious. The next day, they go to the police in the nearby town. The authorities thank them for the information.

The local researchers are not sure anything will change. They say that often the logging companies pay off the police to leave them alone. But for now, you feel good. You've done the right thing.

THE END

To read another adventure, turn to page 9.
To learn more about Tropical Rain Forests, turn to page 101.

Africa's mountain gorillas are one of the world's most endangered species. There are only about 1,000 total gorillas living in the wild.

CHAPTER 4
ANIMAL RESEARCH

You are thrilled for the chance to work with these animals. Concerns about declining animal species is one of the reasons you studied tropical forests in the first place.

The sad part is that humans have caused a lot of animal species to become endangered or extinct. People destroy animal habitats by farming, raising livestock, mining, logging, and development. Pollution, pesticides, hunting, and fishing also affect animal populations.

One of the biggest things that hurts these animals is climate change, which is caused mainly by burning fossil fuels. People are adding carbon dioxide to the atmosphere at a rate faster than any other time in history.

Turn the page.

The extra carbon dioxide traps heat and raises the planet's temperature. This changes the weather and habitats. And it is resulting in the loss of animal species all over the world, from insects and toads to birds and big cats.

You hope your skills as a researcher will help the team understand these losses—and maybe even prevent some of them.

Eddie and his team have two projects that you can join. One is right here in Panama. Researchers are studying the local bat populations, which have been mysteriously declining. You will crawl into caves to learn about these fascinating creatures.

The other project is happening on the other side of the South Atlantic Ocean. In the Democratic Republic of the Congo, poachers

Dark caves are home to several species of bats in rain forests around the world.

have been hunting forest elephants. You will monitor the elephant population while possibly coming face-to-face with armed hunters.

To study bats in Panama, turn to page 70.

To study elephants in the Democratic Republic of the Congo, turn to page 72.

You have always been interested in bats. They are important as well as fascinating. Vampire bats live in this area. These bats feed on the blood of mammals. They have been useful for developing medicines to treat blood clots and strokes.

In the morning, you and Eddie join another researcher named Donna. She lays her head back against the seat of the Jeep to get a little rest, her eyes hidden behind sunglasses, as Eddie drives you to your research location.

A couple hours later, you reach a wall of trees and underbrush. The three of you strap on your packs and hike into the woods. The air buzzes with the sound of flying insects. Eddie slashes the brush with a machete as you go deeper into the rough. Howler monkeys howl in the distance. Exotic birds call to one another.

Soon, you hear water running over rocks. Eddie follows it to a creek.

"Here," Eddie says, checking the GPS. He points to an opening in the ground about the size of a manhole. "This where the bats come out at nightfall. That's our entry point."

Eddie says he is going upstream to look for other entry points. That leaves you and Donna to explore the cave.

To crawl into the cave first, turn to page 76.
To leave the job to Donna, turn to page 78.

The decision is easy for you. How can you pass up the chance to go to Africa? On the long journey to the Democratic Republic of the Congo, Eddie tells you and the other team members about the project you'll be doing there.

The Democratic Republic of the Congo is home to forest elephants. They play a critical role in keeping the rain forest—and the planet—healthy. As they clomp around the forest, these elephants eat small, softwood trees and smash down small trees and bushes with their feet.

By eating and crushing smaller plants, the elephants leave more space, water, and nutrients for the bigger trees to grow. Those large, slow-growing hardwood trees are the key to fighting climate change. They store huge amounts of carbon dioxide, keeping it out of the atmosphere.

Turn the page.

Elephants play an important role in helping rain forest trees grow large and strong. The trees in turn provide homes and food for other animals and help reduce greenhouse gases, which helps the whole planet.

But forest elephants are being hunted for their tusks. It's illegal to hunt these elephants. But that doesn't stop poachers from doing it. The tusks can be sold for a lot of money.

"If these elephants die off here, the consequences for the environment would be devastating," Eddie says.

After arriving in the Democratic Republic of the Congo, you team up with a local guide named Mamadou. The three of you ride bicycles along a logging road. Bags with supplies are strapped to the bikes. You head toward an old logging camp a few miles up the road.

"We had reports of poachers in this part of the jungle this morning," Mamadou yells to you as you pedal along. "That means that the elephants are here too," he adds.

A dried-up stream bed crosses the road. Mamadou stops. "This used to run with lots of water," he says. "During this time of year, it should be full."

To keep riding toward the logging camp, turn to page 79.

To hike up the stream bed to see what's wrong, turn to page 82.

"I'll go in," you say.

You strap on your headlamp and pull on your gloves. Then you get down on your stomach in front of the opening. It smells like mud and something rotten. Craning your neck to peer inside, your light lands on a smooth rock passageway. You grab onto the edge of the opening and pull yourself in.

You crawl forward, scanning your surroundings. No sign of any bats yet, but you see a bigger opening up ahead. You crawl toward it. You slip through the second hole and fall five or six feet into a muddy bed. Sitting up, you look around.

You're in an open space about the size of a kitchen. In a nearby corner, a dozen vampire bats hang silently upside down.

Vampire bats are found in several tropical regions with warm and moist climates. They like to live in caves that are very dark.

On the far side of the room, you see another opening. A thick layer of bat droppings covers the ground outside the opening.

To call Donna into the room and conduct your tests here, turn to page 85.

To check out the next room, turn to page 88.

You don't want to look like you're scared, but . . . well, you kind of are.

"You can do it," you say to Donna.

"Thanks a lot," she says sarcastically.

She takes off her cap and puts on her headlamp. Then she disappears inside the cave.

You stand by the opening, listening for Donna's report. Half an hour passes, and you start to get worried. She should have called for you by now. You call inside, but there's no answer. You look around. Eddie is 50 yards up the creek bed.

To go in after Donna alone, turn to page 90.
To go find Eddie for help, turn to page 93.

If there are poachers in the area, they might be staying at the abandoned logging camp. Mamadou leads the way, pedaling his bike over small logs and around an anthill that is taller than him. The old logging road is nearly grown over with plants in some spots. You get off the bikes to push through the brush.

It is late afternoon by the time you reach the old logging camp. At the far end of a small clearing, two flimsy huts with tin roofs face each other. A firepit sits in front of them.

"Look over there," Eddie says, pointing to a tarp-covered bundle the size of a suitcase.

Mamadou kneels by the fire pit. "These ashes are warm," he says.

You realize the camp is not abandoned at all. Someone has been using it. And they could be back any time.

Turn the page.

Eddie lifts the tarp to reveal several elephant tusks. "Oh, no," he says.

Just then, you hear a truck pulling up the road. It turns into the camp and stops, blocking your path.

"Run!" Mamadou yells.

It's believed that each year at least 20,000 elephants are killed in Africa for their tusks. Authorities are working hard to catch the poachers who are illegally killing the mighty animals.

Eddie grabs one of the tusks as you bolt into the woods, leaving the bikes behind. Headlights sweep across the camp. Panic fills your stomach as you hear men yelling and running through the woods after you.

It's very dark in the forest now, but Mamadou knows his way. Soon, you don't hear anyone chasing you. You make it to a nearby town by morning, exhausted and still afraid for your lives.

You go to the police to report the poachers. Eddie shows them the tusk he swiped from the camp. The police vow to investigate.

THE END

To read another adventure, turn to page 9.
To learn more about Tropical Rain Forests, turn to page 101.

You leave the bikes along the side of the road, grab your water bottle, and drop into the stream bed. You walk upstream. Soon you notice large piles of elephant dung along the banks.

"This was their water source and a gathering place," Mamadou says. "But look, the dung is dry and old."

"So the elephants haven't been here lately?" you ask.

"That is how it looks," Mamadou says.

You continue upstream. Within an hour, you hear the sound of rushing water. Finally, you come to a chain-link fence. It goes across the streambed and stretches into the woods. Beyond it is an open field with cattle grazing on grass. After being under the forest canopy for so long, your eyes water at the sight of the bright sky.

Turn the page.

Every year, ranchers clear thousands of acres of rain forest land to make grazing pastures for their cattle.

The sound of running water is coming from somewhere over the rise. You can feel moisture in the air. Nearby, you can see more elephant dung and some broken branches leading into the woods. It's a possible sign that elephants have gone that way. They were probably looking for water.

To climb the fence and investigate, turn to page 95.
To search for the elephants, turn to page 97.

"Donna!" you call. "Come down!"

Donna reaches into the cave and hands you plastic scraping tools and several small plastic bags for collecting samples. Then her hands, face, and shoulders appear in the opening as she squeezes in after you. Soon you're both sitting on cold, damp rock scraping bat droppings into your plastic containers.

After a short while, you hear Eddie outside the cave. You and Donna climb out into the early dusk.

"Let's take a couple of the bats back to the lab," Eddie says.

He strings a thin net across the cave opening. Then you wait. As dusk turns to dark, bats begin to flood out of the opening in a thick wave. Right away, two are caught in the net.

Turn the page.

Wearing leather gloves, Eddie carefully pulls one of the bats out by the feet. You hold open a cotton bag and close it after Eddie slips the squirming creature inside. Then he removes the second bat and puts it in a bag that Donna holds open. As more bats get caught, you repeat the process. By the time you're finished, you've captured eight vampire bats.

Researchers carefully study vampire bats to learn how healthy they are and understand their behavior.

Back at the research center, the team will study the bats' habits. Understanding their social habits may help you find ways to help save the species. Later, you'll attach sensors to their bodies so you can track the bats after they're released. Then you can learn even more about them.

For now, you close your eyes and enjoy the sounds of the forest at night—the croaking frogs, the buzzing insects, the various howls and calls of the wild. It has been a great day, and you can't wait to get back at it again tomorrow.

THE END

To read another adventure, turn to page 9.
To learn more about Tropical Rain Forests, turn to page 101.

You crawl to the other side of the room, then lower yourself into the deeper room. Your headlamp shows this room is much larger than the first—it's the size of a small gymnasium. Hundreds of bats hang above you. On the north end, a trickle of water comes down the wall. The rock is veined with green and rust colors.

"Donna!" you yell back. "Get in here! This is amazing."

Holding plastic tubes under the drip, you and Donna collect several ounces of water. A few of the bats stir, opening their wings, but they stay put.

A few days later, back at the research center, Donna calls you into the lab. "We have results of that water we collected," she says. "It's contaminated."

"With chemicals?" you ask.

She nods. "Pesticides, most likely."

The contaminated water is traced to a vast farm. More tests confirm that the farmers are using illegal chemicals on the crops. Donna calls a local government branch and explains what is happening.

"Nice job, team!" she says after she hangs up.

This won't solve everything for the bats, but you helped make a difference. For now, you feel good about your work—and the future.

THE END

To read another adventure, turn to page 9.
To learn more about Tropical Rain Forests, turn to page 101.

You get down on your stomach and slide headfirst into the cave. Your headlamp splashes across the smooth rock around you as you wriggle inside. Finally, you drop onto a rock shelf. You're in a small room, but there's no sign of Donna.

You crawl toward another opening and into a bigger room. You find Donna lying with her back against a wall. She's breathing hard. Her left pant leg is rolled up past her ankle.

"What's the matter?" you ask.

That's when you notice a long pit viper slithering several feet away. It's a snake known locally as an *equis,* named for the X marks on its back. It is one of the most deadly snakes in Central and South America. You look at Donna's ankle and see bite marks.

Common lancehead snakes are just one of several venomous snakes that live in rain forests around the world.

Quickly, you grab Donna under her arms and pull her across to the opening. Thankfully, the snake has slithered away. But there may be more of them—they must nest here.

Turn the page.

You pull Donna into the first room, then across it to the main opening. She is fading in and out of consciousness. You're starting to worry. It's taking a long time to get her out. How long does it take for the poisonous venom to get to her heart?

You hear Eddie outside the cave, and you call to him. He reaches inside and grabs onto Donna as you heft her up.

Finally, you get Donna outside the cave and quickly drive to the nearest hospital. While you wait to hear a report, Eddie pats you on the back.

"You did good getting Donna out of there," he says.

You nod, but you're not sure. If she dies, you'll blame yourself for taking so long to go after her.

THE END

To read another adventure, turn to page 9.
To learn more about Tropical Rain Forests, turn to page 101.

You run upstream after Eddie and tell him that you haven't heard from Donna. He gets a worried look on his face.

"We need to go in after her," he says.

The two of you go back to the cave entrance. Eddie pulls on a headlamp and slides head first into the hole.

As you wait, you look in the tall grass and see the eyes of dozens of frogs reflecting in your flashlight.

Turn the page.

Small frogs, like this glass frog, live in rain forests across Central and South America.

You know from your studies that these are glass frogs. You can see through their abdomens. It's weird to see such beauty in the midst of an emergency.

Finally you hear Eddie calling from inside the cave. "Get over here!"

You help Eddie pull Donna outside. She's barely conscious.

"She's been bitten by a snake," Eddie says, climbing out after her. "Help me get her into the Jeep. We've got to get her to the hospital now!"

Eddie drives at top speed through the jungle. You hold onto Donna, hoping you can get her help in time. You wish you'd gone in to look for her sooner.

THE END

To read another adventure, turn to page 9.
To learn more about Tropical Rain Forests, turn to page 101.

You toss your packs over the fence and climb over. You walk across the field where the cattle are. The ranchers built a dam to redirect the stream here. The cattle drink from a shallow pond. A pump sprays water over rows of corn and wheat.

"Isn't ranching illegal here?" you ask Mamadou.

He just nods. You can see anger in his face.

"We can't let them get away with this," you say.

That's when Eddie has an idea. The dam is just put together with rocks and mud. You hide until dark. Then you go to the dam and start pulling it apart. Quietly, you heave the rocks into the field.

Turn the page.

Soon, water is flowing slowly around your boots. Eventually it is gushing. You smile, thinking of the elephants and other forest creatures getting their water back.

You climb back over the fence. Your fingers are cut, bloody, and bruised. The ranchers can rebuild the dam, but now your team will know if they do. Maybe this is what it means to fight for tropical forests—small gains and losses. As you set up camp that night, you feel good. You feel like you can make a difference in the world.

THE END

To read another adventure, turn to page 9.
To learn more about Tropical Rain Forests, turn to page 101.

You don't like the look of this place. A big ranching operation like that is probably protected by people with guns. So you turn back and follow the trail.

Finally, near dusk, you come across some forest elephants chewing on some leafy ferns. They are smaller than savannah elephants, but they are still big. They weigh thousands of pounds. They are awesome.

As you watch, two elephants finish chewing and begin to play. They rear up on their hind legs and clash. They trample the bushes and make snuffling sounds with their trunks. Eddie snaps dozens of photos.

Eventually the elephants finish their game and walk away. You trail them. You hope they'll lead you to more. You can tag them

Turn the page.

Forest elephants often stay cool in lakes, rivers, and streams.

with electronic sensors so you can track the herd. As you follow behind the elephants, you can't help smiling. Working in a tropical rain forest is as fun and fulfilling as you dreamed it would be.

THE END

To read another adventure, turn to page 9.
To learn more about Tropical Rain Forests, turn to page 101.

The flying animals in a rain forest, such as bats, birds, and butterflies, mainly live among the tallest trees, which make up the forest's emergent layer.

CHAPTER 5

TROPICAL FORESTS

Tropical forests are one of two main types of rain forest. These forests have lots of trees and huge amounts of rainfall. Tropical forests are found near the equator in South America, Central America, Mexico, Africa, Asia, and Australia.

Tropical forests receive about 14 feet (2 meters) of rainfall each year. They are consistently hot, with temperatures ranging between 68 and 95 degrees Fahrenheit (20 and 35 degrees Celsius).

Like all rain forests, tropical forests are made up of four layers. The emergent layer is where the tallest trees poke out above the canopy. They can be 200 feet (61 m) tall.

The canopy is about 20 feet (6 m) thick and is the busiest part of the forest. It is home to the vast majority of the forest's animals, including birds, apes, insects, and many more. It also has a wide variety of flowers and fruits. The tops of the trees in the canopy join together, forming a roof that blocks most of the sunlight from reaching into the lower parts of the forest.

Below the canopy is the understory. This is a layer of shrubs, ferns, and smaller trees that do not touch each other. At the bottom is the forest floor, where very few plants grow because of the lack of sunlight. It is hot and wet on the forest floor.

Tropical forests are home to about half of the world's plants and animals, including more kinds of trees than any other forests in the world. Their large, hardwood trees clean a huge amount of the world's air, storing carbon dioxide and making oxygen. The forests produce and filter water, and have many plants that are used to make medicines.

But tropical forests are endangered. Logging companies cut down the trees for timber. Farmers and ranchers clear the forest to raise crops and livestock. The Amazon has lost about one-fifth of its rain forest over the past 40 years. These losses take away habitats for many of the species that live there, including many endangered animals. They also make climate change worse by taking away the big trees that store carbon dioxide.

Environmental groups realize how important rain forests are to Earth's future. Each year, they work to plant hundreds of thousands of new trees to try to restore lost forest land.

Many global organizations, activist groups, and governments are working to protect tropical forests. They fight against illegal logging and poaching. Other groups plant trees, work to

protect wildlife, and create ecotourism vacations,
where tourists can visit tropical forests and spend
money to contribute to their protection.

SHRINKING HOMELAND

Rain forests are home to thousands of animal species. But many species are threatened by the loss of millions of acres of rain forest each year. If the destruction of rain forests continues, many of these animals may become extinct.

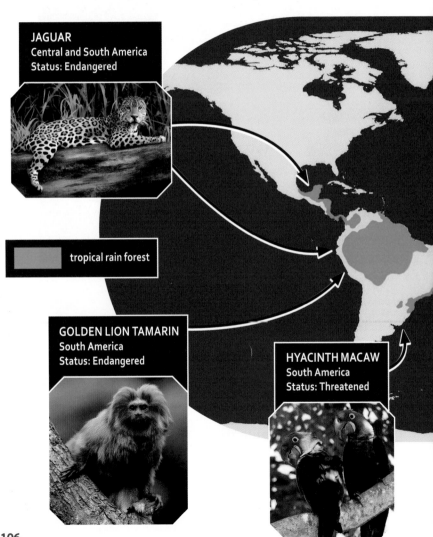

JAGUAR
Central and South America
Status: Endangered

tropical rain forest

GOLDEN LION TAMARIN
South America
Status: Endangered

HYACINTH MACAW
South America
Status: Threatened

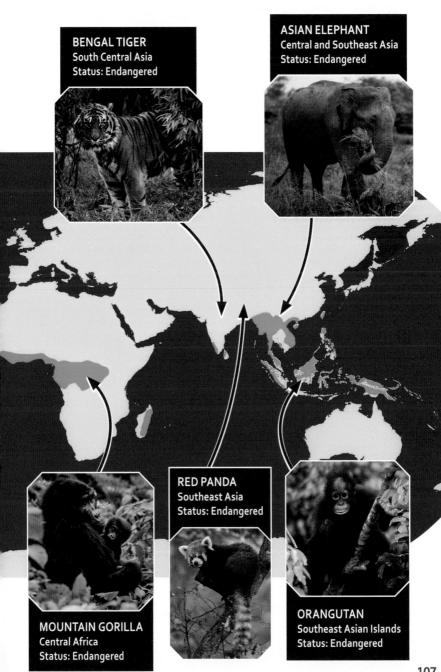

BENGAL TIGER
South Central Asia
Status: Endangered

ASIAN ELEPHANT
Central and Southeast Asia
Status: Endangered

RED PANDA
Southeast Asia
Status: Endangered

MOUNTAIN GORILLA
Central Africa
Status: Endangered

ORANGUTAN
Southeast Asian Islands
Status: Endangered

GLOSSARY

bonobo (buh-NOH-bow)—an ape with a black face and black hair, found in the rain forests of the Democratic Republic of the Congo

canopy (KA-nuh-pee)—the middle layer of the rain forest where the greenery is thick and there is little sunlight

carbon dioxide (KAHR-buhn dy-AHK-syd)— a colorless, odorless gas that people and animals breathe out; plants take in carbon dioxide

dung (DUHNG)—solid waste from animals

ecosystem (EE-koh-sis-tuhm)—a system of living and nonliving things in an environment

endangered (in-DAYN-juhrd)—at risk of dying out

firebreak (FYR-brayk)—a gap, such as a strip of open space, that acts as a barrier to slow or stop the progress of a wildfire

fire retardant (FYR ruh-TAAR-duhnt)—chemicals that firefighters spread from air tankers in order to keep a wildfire from spreading

fossil fuel (FAH-suhl FYOOL)—a natural fuel formed from the remains of plants and animals; coal, oil, and natural gas are fossil fuels

habitat (HAB-uh-tat)—the natural place and conditions in which an animal lives

livestock (LYV-stok)—farm animals

machete (muh-SHEH-tee)—long, heavy knife with a broad blade that can be used as a tool or as a weapon

mammal (MAM-uhl)—a warm-blooded animal that breathes air; mammals have hair or fur

militia (muh-LISH-uh)—a group of volunteer citizens who are organized to fight, but who are not professional soldiers

poacher (POHCH-ur)—a person who hunts or fishes illegally

species (SPEE-sheez)—a group of plants or animals that share common characteristics

tanker (TANK-ur)—an airplane equipped with tanks for carrying liquids

tusk (TUHSK)—one of the pair of long, curved, pointed teeth of an elephant, walrus, wild boar, or other animal

venom (VEN-uhm)—a poison made by some snakes; snakes inject venom

OTHER PATHS TO EXPLORE

>>> In one story path, you work to put out a fire in the rain forest. What would you do if you discovered a wild animal that was injured in the fire? Would you try to help it?

>>> When you're in the Democratic Republic of the Congo in Africa, you set up cameras to capture photos of wild animals living in the area. If you were in the Congo region, what kind of animals would you like to research? What is the one animal you would like to see up close?

>>> While researching wild forest elephants, you discover a hidden pile of illegal elephant tusks. What would you do if you learned that elephants were being killed illegally? How could you help protect forest elephants from being killed by poachers?

READ MORE

Gibbs, Maddie. *What Are Tropical Rainforests?* New York: Britannica Educational Publishing, 2019.

Iyer, Rani. *Endangered Rain Forests: Investigating Rain Forests in Crisis.* North Mankato, MN: Capstone Press, 2015.

Vonder Brink, Tracy. *Protecting the Amazon Rainforest.* Lake Elmo, MN: Focus Readers, 2020.

INTERNET SITES

National Geographic: Rainforests, Explained
nationalgeographic.com/environment/habitats/rain-forests/#close

Worldwide Fund for Nature (WWF): Tropical Rainforests
wwf.panda.org/our_work/our_focus/forests_practice/importance_forests/tropical_rainforest/

INDEX